BLACK&BOLD

THE ONE

Recognizing the one the soul needs

Jessica Bailey

Contents

Dedication

I dedicate this book to Christopher Wilson, a beacon of wisdom and mentorship. Through your guidance, you have bestowed upon me the foundation to soar to new heights. Your belief in my potential has fuelled my journey, and your teachings have shaped my path in ways I could never have imagined. Thank you for your unwavering support and for being the wind beneath my wings.

To my boys, who endured my absence during Christmas time with grace and understanding. Your patience and understanding during moments of solitude while I penned these pages are deeply appreciated. Your unwavering love and support have been my greatest motivation and source of strength. This book is a tribute to your resilience and a testament to the bond that holds us together, even in moments of separation.

May the worlds you encounter within these pages ignite your own sense of wonder and inspire you to dream beyond the confines of reality. Without your unwavering support and understanding, this journey would not have been possible.

With heartfelt thanks,

Jessica Bailey

February 2024

Chapter 1: Like a sister to Me

I'm retiring to the UK," Richard calmly announces, oblivious to the seismic impact his words are having. Struggling to maintain composure, Tamara paints on a smile as her heart sinks like an anchor. "That's… amazing news," she hears herself utter, the words feeling like pebbles in her throat. Definitely not what she was expecting to hear. "When will you be going?"

"Next month," comes the casual reply, clearly unaware of the tempest brewing within Tamara. Time seems to freeze as the weight of his decision hangs in the air. Nevertheless she, fights to keep the façade intact and continues the conversation, pretending all is well when, in reality, her world has just been shattered.

Trying to mask the emotions swirling within her, she forces a nod and musters a weak smile. "Next month…that's soon," she manages to say, though her voice betrays the internal turmoil. Richard, still oblivious to the tumultuous sea he has just stirred, continues to share details of his impending move.

As he speaks of the UK's allure and the opportunities that await him, Tamara finds herself drifting further away, grappling with the abrupt revelation that their paths are about to diverge. The room, once filled with the hum of everyday conversation, now echoes with the heavy silence of an impending farewell.

As she navigates the rest of the conversation, she's acutely aware that the landscape of her life is about to change, and she's left wondering how to weather the storm that has unexpectedly rolled in.

As she slides into her car and turns the key, Tamara barely hears the engine's purr, drowned out by the echoes of his announcement. She takes a deep breath and attempts to steady herself, but as the car pulls away, the floodgates burst open. Tears stream down her face, a torrent of unspoken emotions washing over her.

The following morning, numb from the previous night's outpouring, she sits on her couch, cradling a cup of untouched coffee. Her swollen eyes bear witness to the hours spent drowning in sorrow, but the weight of the reality presses on her shoulders, leaving her unsettled and vulnerable, unable to swim away. Eventually, she summons up the courage to pull out her phone and dial Richard's number.

"I have a coping mechanism for goodbyes, used it when my father was sick," she confesses. "I leave first, cut contact, so when they go, I've already moved on. I'm going to let you go now."

Silence lingers before Richard responds with a bewildered, "What?!"

"If you're serious about relocating to the UK, then I have to let you go now," she reiterates, her voice cracking despite herself.

"But it's not until next summer!" Richard protests.

"What difference does it make? Potato, *po-tah-to*," she retorts sharply.

"But we could still stay in touch. You're like a sister to me and..." he starts, but his reply is cut short.

"Bye now," she garbles in an instant, and hangs up the phone.

She pauses for a moment. "I'm like a *sister* to him!"

She chuckles with bitter amusement. "Five years of fucking, and I'm like a *sister* to him."

Then, in a fit of rage, she stands, coils, and flings her phone against the wall, smashing it into the same number of pieces as her heart.

Boom mics hover like vigilant sentinels, capturing the heartbeat of the set. Actors, poised for their moment, immerse themselves in their roles as the camera gracefully dances across the scene. It all unfolds seamlessly until, with nothing more than a wave of her hand, Tamara commands "Cut."

Her authoritative voice slashes through the air, signaling the end of the take. "Excellent performance. Let's trash one or two more scenes," she suggests, her energy as palpable as it is tense. The team is momentarily taken aback, and puzzled glances are exchanged. *What did I say wrong?'*

"I think we're going to have to call it a day," interjects the 1st Assistant Director. Tamara's eyebrows knit in confusion. "Why's that? We've still got time; we *could* still trash one more scene," she reiterates, her commitment to the craft evident in her tone.

"We could, except that it's Valentine's Day."

'Right…and?'

"Many of us have lovers to attend to," the 1st AD replies matter-of-factly. This time, the realization does dawn on Tamara – it *is* Valentine's Day, a day meant for love and companionship. The underlying point of the day stings, reminding her that she has no one to share it with.

Later that night, while everyone is gone, Tamara and her cameraman lay on the grass together, the sky presenting a cosmic canvas above them as they share their weed-induced euphoria. In the haze of the night, Tamara, feeling a sense of security, begins to pour out her heart.

"What's wrong with me?" she asks, her words floating into the night. The cameraman, Jason, listens attentively. "What?" he replies, the softness in his voice encouraging her to open up a bit further.

"Why don't I have a man?" she implores to the heavens, her vulnerability exposed in the dim light. Jason shifts, absorbing her words before responding, "I think it's because you just don't want one."

"What?!" Tamara sits up, the weight of his statement sinking in. "You're a beautiful, talented woman, Tamara. A woman like you can get any man she wants," he reassures her. Tamara chews on the words, feeling her pulse lower a bit before replying, quietly, "I guess you might be right." She lies back down.

"What?" Jason replies, the softness in his voice urging her on.

"He says I'm like a *sister* to him," she half chuckles in bitter amusement.

"Five years of swimming through my vagina and I'm like a sister to him.

No clarity. Nothing. I don't even know if he's married. Separated, he *says*, but I don't know his house. Liked him, but he used me. Unbelievable that I've stooped so low." She continues, her words becoming a monologue of despair.

"When you meet someone, clarify in simple terms before committing; don't assume. Lesson learned," she imparts to herself, her words carrying the weight of experience. Jason, reduced to his role of silent confidant, absorbs her tale of emotional bruising.

"I thought we had something. Five years, great connections, and he wants to leave," she continues, her voice sharp with regret. "No regard for my feelings. Who does that?" Her vulnerability hangs in the air so thick that Jason can now almost touch it.

"I must be the stupidest person. I'm usually so smart, but not with this one," she muses. Jason, unmoved, continues to absorb her emotions. "How did I let myself be so stupid? He doesn't even owe me an explanation. I've simply been used for pleasure and dumped. All that sex and all I am is a *sister* to him," she says again, her voice unwavering, but the tears start to stream down her face nonetheless, as she comes to terms with the intimate details of love's unravelling.

"Gotta go," she says suddenly, getting abruptly to her feet and fiddling with her car keys.

"What? You sure?" Jason asks with concern.

"Yup. I'll see you tomorrow."

"Tamara, I can take you home," he offers.

"I'm fine…" she says more forcefully.

But the lie is only too transparent as she trips over herself, stumbles and falls.

Jason rushes over to help and they both pause as a passing siren breaks their train of thought.

They look at each other and Jason says, more insistently,

"I should take you home."

"Yeah," comes the reply, signalling a weary defeat.

Chapter 2: My Dream Man

As she scans the library shelves, Tamara's eyes come to rest on a book entitled "Manifest Your Dream Man". A momentary pause ensues, her fingers lightly grazing the spine of the book. She rolls her eyes, chuckling at the seemingly whimsical idea suggested by the title. Brushing off the notion, she continues her search for the book she originally sought.

At the checkout counter, having finally settled on a scriptwriting book, her phone rings. A voice chatters down the line and she replies brisky, "I'm on my way, Carl, see you in 5," before rushing into her car and turning the key, sending the engine roaring to life.

Upon arrival at the quaint coffee shop, she finds Carl patiently waiting, a warm smile adorning his face. Settling into her seat, she apologizes for her tardiness, to which he graciously responds, "That's okay, you're here now." The two seamlessly segue into discussions about their upcoming project, their words weaving a tapestry of excitement and dedication.

As they delve into the vision, Carl suggests a practical approach. "I'm thinking handheld would save us a heap of time with this project." Tamara nods, but amid their creative talk, she increasingly finds her attention drawn to a mysterious lady in the corner, engrossed in the very book she had dismissed earlier. Despite her efforts to concentrate, the book beckons to her, a silent enigma.

"I've seen that book twice today," she confesses to Carl. Nonchalantly, he glances over. "Oh, it's a good book, very common - my partner has it." They continue their conversation, the throwaway comment swirling inside Tamara's brain as it forms into a tacit acceptance, a permission.

Later, beside a tranquil water pond, she clutches her copy of "Manifest Your Dream Man" tightly, and a lone duck waddles over, captivated by the intriguing woman. As it stands before her, Tamara sighs heavily and before she knows it, she is sharing the complexities of her life. The duck listens, its gaze fixed on her eyes.

"How are you? What's going on with you?" Tamara inquires as the duck moves a little closer, as if it understands her words.

"I'm glad you're okay. Because my life has gone to shit. I'm a sad, lonely woman," she confesses bitterly, pouring out her soul to the attentive duck.

"I mean, I'm successful in my career. I know I am. But I haven't got a man beside me to say, 'well done on all the hard work.' It gets lonely out here," she continues, the vulnerability seeping through her words.

"It never used to be much of a problem, you know. But considering my age, I worry that people like me can only get the leftovers, you know—the potbellied ones," she chuckles. "But apparently not. In fact, this *book*," she waves it towards the duck, causing it to flinch, "this book says otherwise. It says that I can, in fact, attract *any* man that I want." She half-laughs at the irony of the sentence, the pain of recency letting down the confidence of each word.

"That means the whole package, right? The looks, the personality, the attentiveness, the sex…it's all still gettable, right? Not just a never-ending queue of disappointing potbellies?"

She pauses for a bit.

"D'you think that exists?"

Suddenly, a magpie whooshes past her face, startling her. Shooo! Shooo!" she cries, and in a bid to protect herself, she swishes the book at the magpie but loses her grip as she does, and the book leaves her grasp for the apparent sanctity of the pond.

"Definitely not a good sign," Tamara sighs, walking over to the water and rescuing the book, which is now completely soaked. As she stands, her eyes catch the ripples in the pond as they carry her dancing reflection. Worse still, the duck has gone. *Fine, I'll just have to talk to myself,'* she mutters under her breath, wrapping the book up in her coat and marching back to her car.

Back at home, she gets her hairdryer out and fans the pages lightly, causing them to crinkle slightly. Then, fed up with the whole ordeal, she tosses the book onto her desk, letting it settle amongst the many tomes that serve as constant décor to her room before stomping downstairs to put the kettle on.

A couple of months later, Tamara's 40th birthday arrives and she throws a party to try and fill the house with memories and happiness, but as soon as she sees the last attendees off at the end of the night, the closing door echoes with loneliness. There, in the quiet, she still feels nothing but the void.

Alone in her room, she sits on her bed, sobbing and sipping wine. Suddenly, she sees it. "Manifest Your Dream Man" comes back into focus on her desk, a symbol of unfulfilled desires.

In this rare moment of quiet solitude, she cradles the now-dried book in her hands, its pages once more whispering promises of a life transformed. As she flips it open, the first line beckons her attention: "Do you know you have the power to manifest the man that you want?" A spark of intrigue lights up her eyes and with a sense of purpose, she grabs her diary and pen, ready to embark on a journey of self-discovery.

Her hand glides effortlessly across the diary's pages, each stroke narrating the desires of her heart. She gives the notes a heading that boldly declares her intentions: "My Dream Man." The inked words become a canvas on which she can paint the portrait of her ideal partner, each detail etched with precision and passion. She begins a list:

1. Tall – 6 foot

2. Handsome, like a movie star

3. Athletic build

4. White

5. Has children already, so he isn't pestering me to have any.

The list extends, more precisely capturing the essence of her deepest longings and unspoken wishes. The room, bathed in a soft glow, becomes a sanctuary for her quiet dreams as the pen continues to dance across the pages, articulating the unspoken desires of her heart.

Having completed the list, Tamara delicately closes the diary, each page now imbued with the whispered secrets of her soul. By placing the pen on top, she seals this pact with the universe—a covenant of dreams and aspirations that she hopes will transcend into reality. The air in the room shimmers with the weight of possibilities, and Tamara, fueled by a newfound courage, decides in that moment that she will take fate into her own hands.

She scours the internet for a dating app, and when she finally settles on one, she downloads it and opens it up straight away, navigating its virtual realm and meticulously crafting a profile that mirrors the facets of her vibrant personality. Every detail is there, every question answered, and every carefully chosen photo uploaded until she feels she has set the stage for the manifestation of her desires to play out in the tangible world of connections.

After a few hours, she puts down her phone, the room echoing with the lingering resonance of her quiet dreams and unspoken longings. A fragile symphony of hope and anticipation hovers in the air, promising a tomorrow adorned with the possibilities of love. Her journey into the realm of manifestation having begun, she quickly succumbs to the embrace of sleep with assurance anew, eagerly anticipating a new day ripe with the potential to read out loud the chapters of her heart's desires.

Chapter 3: Love Calling

In the quiet sanctuary of her dimly lit room, Tamara finds herself engrossed in the final draft of her script, a masterful dance of creativity unfolding on the glowing canvas of her computer screen. The room becomes a cocoon of inspiration, with the soft hum of mental activity permeating the air around her. Ideas flow seamlessly from her mind to the fingertips, bringing the narrative to life.

Amidst the solitary symphony of key taps and the warm glow of the computer screen, Tamara's phone interrupts the creative flow with a series of insistent beeps. Initially dismissing the distractions, she can't resist the allure of curiosity. Opening her phone, she discovers a string of text messages on a dating app, each notification vying for her attention.

The message that catches her eye is from Oliva, who is expressing the hope of getting to know her better. However, Tamara is too immersed in her creative endeavor, so she briefly glances at his profile and decides not to engage at that moment. The pull of her script proves stronger than the potential connection, and she returns to her writing, the room still offering up a hive of inspiration.

Night descends, and once again, Tamara's phone beckons her. Opening the app, she engages with Oliva's message before surrendering to the embrace of sleep. The next morning arrives with a soft glow, and another "good morning" message from the same man graces her screen. This time, he is requesting her number, citing work restrictions on the dating app.

Tamara chuckles at the ploy but provides her number, nonetheless. Returning to Oliva's profile, she studies his photos. Perhaps he isn't what you'd call 'conventionally attractive,' but a certain intrigue lingers. As she scrolls through, she sees his answers to some of the questions on his profile. One in particular grabs her: in response to "Who do you call if you have a problem?" His response, "I call my sister and she always offers me comfort," draws a smile, softening Tamara's initial reservations.

The night brings forth another message from Oliva, this time wishing her a good night's sleep. Tamara contemplates her response before replying, initiating a steady stream of conversation. She cuts to the chase straight away. "Sorry if I'm being too direct, but to save each other's time, d'you mind sharing your profile details like, age, height, weight, et cetera... it just saves time, if you know what I mean." She is surprised to get an immediate reply: "Absolutely." I like direct, so no need to apologize."

To her disbelief, the details he shares align flawlessly with her concept of a dream man: an imposing 184 cm tall, 42 years old, two children, and considerable athleticism. The accompanying photos paint a vivid picture of an individual who could effortlessly grace the cover of a fitness magazine. His handsome features are accentuated by a broad smile that gives way to stunning dimples, adding an endearing charm. His eyes captivate her with an alluring depth.

As the images flicker on Tamara's screen, her eyes widen with shock, and a gasp escapes her lips. She checks her list and realizes he's ticked them all off. *'This can't be real.'* It's as if the universe has cleverly orchestrated this surreal alignment. Balancing herself, she composes a reply, her fingers dancing across the keyboard while she tries to conceal the excitement that is radiating through her.

She decides to reveal her own profile details – 40 years old, 175cm tall. A momentary hesitation lingers as she contemplates sharing her weight. Then, she types out 60KG, before hesitating, doubting her decision. She deletes it and tries 65kg to see what it looks like, but erases it again.

Finally, with a resolute decision, she settles on 60kg, a declaration she pairs with a search for the perfect photos in her album. Scrolling through recent captures, though, she finds them lacking. Moving to the top, a triumphant "yup" escapes her lips as she discovers the ideal one – a photo that aligns seamlessly with the weight she has declared. With a swift press of a button, she sends off her curated collection.

As the images reach Oliva, his response is swift, a virtual whisper that lingers in the digital air: "You have a gorgeous smile." A fluttering warmth fills Tamara's chest. "They're my magical charm," she replies. "Whatever you do, don't tamper with my smiles." I'll do my best to keep them shiny," Oliva assures her playfully. The dance of their digital connection takes on a romantic rhythm, setting the stage for a love story to unfold through their screens.

As their conversation deepens, the exchange of profiles evolves into a captivating visual journey through their lives. Tamara exudes confidence as she shares carefully selected photos, each image serving as a testament to the joy and vitality that this man could bring into her world. A swift acknowledgment signals the birth of a connection, and the room seems to pulse with the energy of newfound romance.

As the sun sets, Tamara effortlessly slides into the rhythm of night. Oliva's presence occupies her thoughts like a catchy tune, and the engagement between them evolves into an all-encompassing whirlwind of emotions. Their digital dialogs transcend the ordinary, transforming into virtual embraces that echo with the infectious melody of her laughter, and the tangible warmth of their blossoming connection.

Phone calls abound, and chats flow endlessly—questions about meals, outfits, and the everyday minutiae become the threads that weave together their digital tapestry. "What did you eat today?" "What are you wearing?" Each query serves as a delightful note in their symphony of conversation. Daily pictures of their lives dance across their screens, sharing glimpses of both the mundane and the extraordinary.

In this digital waltz, Tamara immerses herself further into the world of the stranger she has yet to meet. The pixels on her screen become windows into his world, creating a kaleidoscope of shared experiences and unspoken connections.

The anticipation builds with each passing day, as the virtual closeness propels them toward the eagerly awaited moment when the screen barriers will dissolve, and their worlds will finally collide.

Oblivious to the passing time and the world beyond her digital sphere, Tamara inhales deeply, savoring the promise of a love that will surely evolve from the virtual to the tangible. As Oliva continues his work away from home, the connection between them intensifies. Love has not just knocked; it has confidently walked through the open door and Tamara has eagerly met its tender embrace.

In the midst of this blossoming love story, she finds herself in a quaint café one afternoon, sharing lunch with an old friend, Marcus. The atmosphere is light, the clinking of cutlery and the murmur of conversations providing the backdrop to their reunion. As Marcus observes her, he senses a change, a certain effervescence that wasn't there before.

"There's something bubbling up around you," his remarks, his eyes studying Tamara's animated expression.

A burst of excitement escapes her lips: "I've found love!"

Marcus leans in, intrigued, "No way! How did you two meet?"

"Online," Tamara reveals, her eyes sparkling with the thrill of her revelation.

Marcus pulls back with a hint of scepticism, cautioning, "Well, be careful. There are many stories out there about the dangers of meeting people online." Then, he smiles and adds, "But of course I'm happy for you. So, have you met in person?"

Tamara, undeterred, offers her reassurance. "Umm...he works away—oil and gas, but he's coming back in three weeks to fully settle here." Her confidence remains steadfast.

"Sounds like he means business," Marcus observes.

"Yup," she affirms, a smile playing on her lips. Leaning in conspiratorially, she whispers in Marcus's ear, "I think this one could be 'the one'".

Marcus smiles, his scepticism fading, replaced by the warmth of his friend's happiness. The café becomes witness to the unfolding chapters of Tamara's unexpected, vibrant love story, each moment painted with the hues of connection, friendship, and the promise of newfound love.

Just before she leaves the café, her screen lights up, right on cue, displaying the words, "I'll be back in Perth in 3 weeks—land on the 17th, a date on the 18th—how's that?"

A feeling of effervescent joy surges through Tamara— *It's happening! It's really happening!* The prospect of a date with her prince charming and the culmination of weeks of virtual connection, fills the car with an ethereal glow. With a swift turn of the key, her car's engine fires into life and she zooms off, enveloped in the stirring melody of a Celine Dion love song.

Chapter 4: My Sexy Self

Tamara's face falls as she sees the scales displaying a mocking "70kg." A stark contrast to what she had told Oliva. Panic sets in—how on earth is she going to shed 10kg? She realizes that she has sat for too long on the couch, writing and eating junk food on set, that she has forgotten to care for herself. In the quiet solitude of her bathroom, she confronts her reflection, a critical eye assessing every curve and contour.

Displeasure marks her expression, particularly as she fixates on that stubborn belly of hers, littered with stretch marks that seem to resist the morning light, hinting at indulgences to which she now wishes she hadn't succumbed. She turns, scrutinizing her backside with such dissatisfaction that it sparks a resolution. She sucks her belly in with an almighty inward breath, then lets it back out. *'Nah, this has to go.'*

With unwavering resolve, she makes the bold decision to start a daily jogging routine, set on shaping her body into living proof of her aspirations – and her testimony. The hours unfold in a montage of sweat and determination, a visual symphony of her relentless pursuit of fitness.

In the theater of her mind, she paints a vibrant picture of herself as a magnetic force, pulling Oliva's gaze with the allure of her newly empowered self. A touch of humor accompanies her musings, entertaining the notion that a guy as handsome as him must have tastes that reach heights as lofty as the heavens. And with this whimsical insight, a clear mission unfolds to match up to the same captivating allure that he must surely crave.

This is no casual endeavor; it's a challenge that Tamara embraces with gusto. She's not in the game to lose; she's here to claim victory over Oliva's heart. After all, she is a master at getting anything she sets her sights on, and she isn't about to let Oliva interrupt her winning streak. The chase is on, and her infectious determination infuses the pursuit with a sense of fun and excitement, turning the romantic journey into a delightful game of hearts.

A week elapses, and with anticipation tinged with nervous excitement, she steps onto the scales. Hope and trepidation dance in her eyes as she awaits the digital revelation. The disappointment is palpable when the numbers remain unchanged, still teasing her with their distinctness. The initial frustration threatens to swell into despair, but the thought of Oliva's imminent arrival proves a potent motivator.

Frustrated yet undeterred, she delves back into the digital realm, fervently seeking ways to expedite this weight loss journey. She dedicates her mornings to following rigorous home workout guides found on YouTube, each movement only fueling her determination. The local fruit and vegetable store becomes her haven, brimming with produce that screams health and vitality.

The days unfold in a disciplined rhythm of jogging and nutrient-packed meals. She'd better hurry up—Oliva would be with her in less than two weeks. Broccoli and cauliflower become the staples of her diet, accompanied by meticulously crafted smoothies. Yet another weigh-in brings forth a disheartening revelation – the numbers on the scale again refusing to budge significantly.

In search of a solution, she turns to her doctor, hoping for a magic fix. With a touch of empathy, he suggests increasing her running time, while emphasizing the uphill battle against weight loss as one navigates the journey of ageing. She is about to leave, crestfallen, when her hope is rekindled by the recommendation of a book, presented to her on a piece of paper in the doctor's scrawled writing. The following day sees her armed with nutritional wisdom, measuring and preparing her meals according to the book's guidance.

Run, healthy food, run, healthy food – her days become a disciplined dance, an unwavering commitment to her goal. Sure enough, her progress does now become evident on the scale, and by the following week, she is able to revel in the triumph of dropping from a size 12 to a size 10. This once-unlikely transformation fuels her confidence, and she stands ready to face Oliva with the radiance of her reshaped self.

Tomorrow would be 'D-day,' the highly anticipated moment when she would finally get to put a face to the man behind the screen, the man who has so stealthily captured her heart. Eager to make a lasting impression, Tamara is on a mission to present her best self in every possible manner. She carefully chooses her outfit, scouring the shops until she spots the perfect dress—her discerning eye instantly understanding exactly what she wants.

With the dress secured, she moves on to makeup, determined to find the ideal foundation and the perfect shades to enhance her features. She lets out a nervous, "I hardly wear makeup, you know."

The makeup artist, intrigued, quips, "Oh, so what's the occasion?"

With a blush, Tamara reveals, "I have a date."

The enthusiastic reply comes: "How exciting! Gotta impress, right?"

As Tamara admires herself in the mirror, she's undeniably pleased. The stunning finish and the breathtaking blush create an orange glow on her caramel cheeks. Confidently, she declares, "Let's go with this."

The makeup artist nods and steps away. Tamara waits anxiously, but when the lady returns, it's bad news.

"We unfortunately don't have any in stock at the moment," she admits, leaving Tamara disappointed.

Undeterred, she says, "Could you give me the name so that I can check your other stores?"

The lady's face flushes, and she hesitates before replying, " It's, um, 'Orgasm.'"

"What?!"

"The name is 'Orgasm.'" Tamara bursts out laughing at the unexpected revelation, thanks the woman and leaves.

As night falls, she can hardly contain her anticipation. Sleep becomes a welcome prospect, a bridge to the momentous day that awaits her. The eagerness to meet Oliva and unveil his mysteries resonates with every heartbeat as she drifts off into the realm of dreams.

When the day arrives, it marks exactly a month since their first conversation. Tamara realizes that it could make or break the beautiful nucleus of their budding relationship, and she crosses her fingers for a positive outcome.

As the evening descends, she stands in her bathroom, palpable excitement radiating from her every move. Following the guidance of a YouTube makeup tutorial, she diligently applies her foundation, the anticipation building with each stroke. A final touch of Orgasm, and calamity strikes—the makeup crashes onto the pristine white tiles, momentarily creating chaos.

Frustration threatens to take over, but just as she is teetering on the edge of releasing her anger, her phone beeps with a text from Oliva. He's equally excited to see her and sharing that he has just had a haircut. The thought of this shared effort to prepare for the night ahead creates a connection and acts as a soothing balm. Tamara can't help but smile—they both want this.

The mutual feeling of anticipation blossoms as she immerses herself in Oliva's photos on her phone, his handsome features and infectious smiles filling her screen. Grateful for her fortune, she zooms in on one, planting a virtual kiss on his lips. "You're mine, baby," she whispers, her excitement soaring.

Under the night's cloak, with the remnants of the sun's warmth fading on the horizon, Tamara guides her car into the cafe driveway. A symphony of fear and excitement dances across her expressions, her face a canvas painted with the hues of anticipation. She's five minutes early and the clock slows to a glacial tick as the appointed time for their date, 7 o'clock, approaches. A moment of suspended stillness prevails—Tamara's heart pounds, taking and exhaling one deep breath as if the universe itself is about to pause to witness this pivotal encounter.

Tamara raises her head and…

…It's him!!!

Chapter 5: Don't Wake Me

Within the cocoon of her car, Tamara's eyes are drawn to a tall figure cloaked in an elegant greyish trench coat. The dimly lit ambiance accentuates his silhouette, and an electric mixture of fear and excitement courses through her. *'This is it,'* she muses, her heart leaping in acknowledgment. From a distance, she studies the handsome stranger, his face catching the moonlight, and her heartbeat quickens in response.

Each feature is well-molded, as if carefully crafted by a designer's touch. His chiseled jawline, deep-set eyes, and the hint of mystery in his expression add layers to the intrigue. As the moonlight traces the lines of his face, Tamara's heartbeat quickens, captivated by the charisma emanating from the captivating figure in the night.

He steps out of a Toyota wagon, his own gait mirroring Tamara's nerves. As he paces around, she observes him with a heightened pulse. When his trajectory brings him closer to Tamara's parked car, she instinctively slides down, seeking refuge in the shadows, her pulse pounding in her ears.

The mysterious man retraces his steps, pulling out a cigarette - or perhaps a cigar - the ember flickering like a beacon in the night. In the halo of the cafe's entrance, he inhales, exhaling tendrils of smoke, a silent ritual to calm his own nerves. Positioned by the door, he awaits her, unaware of her discreet observation.

Summoning her courage, Tamara seizes her bag and steps out into the night. She moves with a quiet elegance, determined to be the queen that she is—a force in her own right. The beating of their hearts echoes in synchronicity in the night air, the suspense tangible. As she approaches, the scene unfolds like a clandestine dance. "Olivia?" she ventures.

"Tamara?" he responds, and a laugh breaks out between them as they bridge the gap and embrace. No doubt, they both like what they see—or so it appears—and they are both very much ready to delve in. The night, having borne witness to their clandestine meeting, envelopes them in its shroud of mystery, as their two hearts meet in laughter and the promise of connection.

He opens the door for Tamara, a gesture of chivalry that ushers her into the enchanting world beyond—a true gentleman. Once they are seated across from each other on this spellbinding night, their eyes meet for the first time, and it's as if the universe erupts into a breathtaking display of instant fireworks.

The palpable chemistry, an electric current passing between them, is not lost on the attentive waitstaff, who silently bear witness to the magnetic connection unfolding before their eyes. As they lock eyes, a cascade of emotions washes over Oliva, who is clearly smitten by Tamara's beauty, confidence, and the broad, charming smile that graces her lips. Upon his gaze, a silent question lingers: "Where have you been all my life?"

Oliva cracks jokes and sends Tamara into fits of laughter, but he also proves to be a good listener, a quality that complements her chattiness, which is particularly heightened when she feels comfortable with someone.

The ambiance is set, and just in time, the Margaret River red wine arrives, releasing its heady aromas into the air—fragrances previously unknown to them both. As they sip the rich nectar, Tamara suddenly pauses, her attention caught by the song playing in the background— it's a rare, native song, definitely not something from this part of the world.

"Wait…is that…?" she begins, her eyes lighting up with recognition.

Oliva leans in, his curiosity piqued. "What?"

"That's Ali playing in the background. That's my song, my favorite…"

A spark of realization glimmers across her face, and Tamara eyes him with a mix of suspicion and amusement. "*You* did this."

Oliva feigns innocence. "Did what?"

"You told them to play my favorite song."

A grin tugs at his lips, but he maintains his innocence. "I didn't do anything."

Tamara remains unconvinced, but with a dead serious expression, he insists, "Must be the universe."

A sigh of contentment escapes her lips, accompanied by a smile. For the first time, someone else has affirmed the presence of the universe in her life, and in that moment, she feels a profound connection. It's the signal she has been waiting for; she needs no further confirmation.

Exhaling with gratitude, she takes a moment to study once more what she would undoubtedly call, "a work of art" standing before her. It's as if he's been crafted and delivered specifically to her from heaven. In that instant, she experiences an overwhelming acknowledgment of just how incredibly fortunate she is.

The universe, with its unseen hands, seems to have orchestrated this meeting, weaving a tapestry of destiny that now unfolds before her. His presence, his aura, it all feels divinely aligned with her deepest desires.

As she observes him, she feels that he, too, is clearly captivated by her, as his eyes soften in color, revealing to her the depth of his feelings. As they stand on the threshold of this shared experience, an unspoken wish lingers in Tamara's heart– the fervent desire that this night could somehow defy the passage of time, allowing them to revel in the magic of their connection for just a little longer. If only time could stand still.

They continue chatting and sip on the wine, both actions intoxicating them equally, awakening senses that didn't exist before. The butterflies in Tamara's stomach are now alive, bubbling and fluttering as she feels the last drops touch her lips, and the eagerness to taste his become irresistible.

With a glance and a subtle gesture, they make their way to the counter. Oliva gracefully pulls out his card and settles the bill at the counter, even leaving a tip for the waiters on their way out.

As they drive closer to the beach in Oliva's car, the moon casts its silvery glow upon the waves, and as they arrive, he gently exits, crosses in front of the bonnet and opens her door. The sea breeze kisses their faces as they stand on the edge of the world, and in that moment, he leans in. Their lips, succulent and eager, meet in a kiss that feels like a surrender. Tamara does just that, and their bodies and lives yield to the enchantment of this moment.

It's not just a kiss; it's a journey into an undiscovered realm of passion. Thirty minutes pass, and they're still exploring each other, their connection deepening with every lingering touch. After a moment, Oliva pauses, his gaze wandering into the distance, leaving Tamara with a sense of curiosity. Something seems to be on his mind, and there is a subtle shift in the air. Concerned, she gently inquires, "Are you okay?"

"Yep," Oliva brushes it off with a nod, but a hint of mystery lingers in his eyes.

"Just thinking how beautiful you are," he finally confesses, and his words hang in the air for her like a soft melody. She blushes at the unexpected compliment, her heart dancing to the sweet rhythm of his words. As she leans her head on his broad chest, he wraps his arms around her, creating a cocoon of warmth and comfort. It's the kind of declaration every woman yearns to hear, yet Tamara, despite feeling the same way, hesitates to reciprocate so soon.

"You are so beautiful," he whispers into her soft ears, his words a gentle caress that ignites a spark between them. In response, Tamara raises her head, locking eyes with him in a silent acknowledgment that passes between them.

She leans in, their lips meeting once more in a passionate dance, tongues entwining as they continue to learn this unspoken language. Hands, soft and gentle, trace the contours of each other's faces, leaving an imprint of desire that lingers long after the kiss ends.

In this sacred space, surrounded by the rhythmic lull of the ocean, they embark on a journey and with each passing moment, the magic of their connection deepens, and the night becomes a canvas painted with the hues of newfound love and shared desire.

Upon returning home, still basking in the glow of the enchanting evening, Tamara sends him a heartfelt message: "Thank you for tonight, I had fun." Almost instantly, his response appears, carrying the warmth of their shared moments: "Me too. Sleep well, and I can't wait for our next date." With a contented smile, she embraces the promise of more delightful moments in the chapters that are yet to unfold.

Chapter 6: Ready When You Are

The sun rises on the morning after their magical first date, and Tamara, eager as always, sends Oliva her familiar "Good morning" text, a ritual that has become the heartbeat of their daily connection. But today is different—no immediate response from Oliva. As minutes turn into hours, a subtle worry creeps into her mind, casting a shadow on the joyous expectation that usually accompanies their morning exchanges.

The uncertainty bleeds into the day, and she finds herself full of anticipation. They had been planning their second date, and Tamara finds herself waiting, her heart pounding in rhythm with the ticking clock. Her eyes remain glued to her phone, seeking the comforting reassurance of Oliva's words.

Finally, in the midst of her apprehension, a chime announces his response. Relief washes over her as she reads his explanation—a genuine delay caused by family matters. Instantly, any trace of worry dissipates and is replaced by a deep understanding and forgiveness. Her trust remains steadfast, and with his text, her day instantly transforms into a canvas painted with the promise of joy.

"I can't wait to see you tonight." Oliva's words act like a balm to Tamara's earlier concerns. Her smile returns, one that radiates warmth and gratitude. As a visual affirmation, he shares a series of photos capturing his ongoing activities, offering her a captivating glimpse into his world. Groceries neatly arranged, heaps of laundry awaiting attention, and a bedroom displaying controlled chaos—essentially, a snapshot of a bachelor's life. Tamara can't help but smile at the charming chaos of it all. The connection between them, tested momentarily, emerges even more strongly in her mind, and the day continues with a renewed sense of excitement and possibility.

Evening falls, and as she applies the finishing touches to her makeup touches, the doorbell's soft melody reverberates through her apartment, heralding Oliva's arrival. Excitement lights up Tamara's eyes as she rushes to open the door, already feeling the warmth of their connection.

A warm hug and as always, Oliva opens the car for her. Ever the gentleman. As they drive off, she finds an evening illuminated by city lights and an uncharted territory that, nevertheless, promises shared laughter and intimate conversations.

Their journey unfolds in the car as it navigates the city's arteries, all aglow with streetlights. Laughter echoes in their private confined space, mingling with the hum of the engine. The dashboard lights cast a gentle glow, painting their faces with a soft warmth that mirrors the blossoming connection between them. The arrival at the restaurant brings with it a tapestry of sophistication, bathed in ambient lights and alive with the clinking of cutlery.

The culinary symphony of the evening unfolds in a cosy ambience, setting the stage for a delightful exploration of flavors and emotions. The carefully chosen red wine, with its velvety richness, becomes the elixir of shared moments, echoing the depth of their growing connection.

As they clink glasses, the resonance of their laughter fills the air, creating an atmosphere of shared joy. Tamara senses a shift in his openness, and gracefully steers the conversation towards the heart of their connection.

"When I was married, we never sat down together and laughed like couples should—we were like two strangers living together," Oliva confesses, laying bare his own vulnerabilities as a layer on top of hers.

"That's sad," Tamara responds, her eyes reflecting empathy.

"I know. The sex was good, but..." he trails off, and a shared laugh punctuates the heaviness of his admission.

"At least that's something," she playfully adds, a genuine smile breaking through.

"I guess so," he acknowledges, his eyes holding a mixture of regret and newfound clarity.

The night unfolds, weaving a shimmering tapestry of shared laughter and meaningful conversation. As they delve into each other's personalities, Tamara finds herself sharing more of her vulnerability with him, spurred on by such a resonant ambience. Oliva's humor leaves her in stitches, particularly as the bottle of wine approaches its end and he gestures to refill her glass, a mischievous glint in his eyes. She waves him off, but he winks and says,

"But how else are we going to support our local farmers?"

She laughs and he adds, completely deadpan,

"It's for a good cause," a playful twinkle in his eyes.

Tamara bursts out laughing and almost falls off her seat. Oliva, delighted by her reaction, continues to tickle her senses with his humor—a distinctive trait in which he takes immense pride.

"You're a comedian," Tamara compliments him, wiping away tears of laughter.

"I get that a lot."

"You should be on stage."

"Nah! My sister is the outgoing one! I'm the funny one, but only backstage," he smiles, and his modesty adds an extra layer of charm to the evening's unfolding narrative.

He leans in close, his eyes tracing the contours of Tamara's face. The restaurant seems to fade away into the background, leaving just the two of them, immersed in a world of stolen glances and whispered confessions.

To Tamara, the moment feels like a scene from a movie, the cameras rolling in the darkness, their faces etched with emotions. There is something unreal unfolding here, something magical that anyone would wish for.

Post-dinner, the night beckons them into a leisurely stroll towards the water's edge. Finding a secluded spot, they immerse themselves in the tranquillity of the night. The surrounding noises—a gentle symphony of waves, distant laughter, and rustling leaves—become the backdrop to their shared intimacy. Under the moonlight, Oliva's warm embrace and Tamara's head resting on his shoulder paint a picture of silent connection.

He plants gentle kisses on her afro-soft hair, running his fingers through it and allowing her to daydream as they sit in quiet communion. In this moment, she wishes time would stand still, an eternal snapshot of their shared bliss.

After what feels like an eternity, Oliva suggests, "Shall we?" Tamara realizes that she has almost fallen asleep, but musters a dreary "Yup," her smile reflecting the contentment of the moment. Oliva helps her up, and they start making their way back to the car, holding hands and passing by the water.

"It's freezing," Tamara shivers, rubbing her arms for warmth.

"Here." Oliva takes off his trench coat and wraps it around her. "A gentleman indeed," she compliments him.

"My mother raised me well," he replies.

"I owe her a bottle of champagne!" They continue to walk in a comfortable silence, until Tamara's question cuts through the air.

"Tell me, would you jump into that water for one million dollars?" she asks, attempting to lighten the mood.

"I'd do it for ten thousand," Oliva replies, his mischievous grin matching the playful glint in his eyes.

"What?! You're kidding, right?" Tamara is taken aback.

"I'm not. It's just water."

"It's so cold though; it can't be more than 2 degrees!" she exclaims.

"I've spent 20 minutes in an ice bath before. It's good for you," Oliva defends, giving her a nonchalant stare.

They head back to the car, holding hands like lovers do, the romantic narrative continuing among shared laughter, soft touches, and tender kisses. *'Love resides in these moments,'* Tamara thinks to herself.

As Oliva's car comes to a gentle stop in Tamara's driveway, the night hangs in the air, heavy with the shared moments of their date. A lingering kiss, filled with the unspoken promise of more, marks the end of the enchanting night. As Tamara prepares to step out of the car, he insists on walking her to her door, extending the connection just a little longer.

The short journey is accompanied by a comfortable silence, the echoes of their laughter still lingering. As they reach Tamara's door, Oliva wraps her in another warm, long hug. A subtle tension is palpable, and as he holds her, he exhales slowly and deliberately, as if grappling with unspoken thoughts.

"Are you okay?" Tamara asks, her concern evident in her voice.

"Yep, all good," he brushes off the moment, his gaze fixed on her.

With a gentle touch, he lifts her cheek, leaning down to plant a warm kiss. "Night," he whispers, reluctantly letting go as she turns and enters the house.

Tucked up in the comfort of her bed, Tamara's phone lights up with a text. "I had a great time. Can't wait for our next date tomorrow."

Tamara relishes the sentiment, but feeling a bit cheeky, she replies, "Tomorrow? You're a bit eager! Don't you think we should give it a few days, so we can both analyse how we feel so far?"

Oliva's response is swift and playful: "I've had a month to analyse!" Tamara can't help but feel a broad smile creep across her face.

Pausing for a moment, phone in hand, she contemplates the next move. After a brief hesitation, she decides to type, "Wondering when we're going to call this a thing then." Summoning the courage, she hits send, but just before putting down her phone, she gets the reply:

"Ready when you are."

The enchantment of the moment feels both surreal and undeniably real—a stroke of luck that only she could experience. As she finally puts down her phone, she lies back in bed, cradling one of her pillows. In the embrace of her daydreams, she savors this slice of heaven on Earth.

Chapter 7: Please Wake Me

Tamara wakes from her restful night, a content smile playing on her lips after the enchanting date with Oliva. She luxuriously stretches, relishing the anticipation of their third date. Reaching for her phone, she is filled with excitement until she sees that there is no text waiting for her. *'No big deal,'* she thinks. *'Maybe he's still sleeping'* Without dwelling on it, she messages him, "Not sure if we planned the time for tonight? Are you still picking me up?" before happily hopping into the shower, feeling like a bride on her honeymoon.

Midday arrives without a response, and she is visibly worried. While her colleagues work around her, dissecting the story of their latest creation, her mind is elsewhere and she finds herself constantly checking her phone. 1 pm ticks by, and still no word. WhatsApp shows her that he hasn't even opened her message yet. *'Uncharacteristic of him.'* As the clock hits 3 pm, anxiety really sets in. She grabs her bag and leaves the room.

In her car, as the engine starts and her phone beeps – finally, a reply. It's casual, not his usual tone, and skirts around addressing any of Tamara's questions about their date and pickup time. Still, it's something. *'Better than silence.'* He claims to be busy with family matters, again. Tamara takes a deep breath to calm her nerves and sends another text, reiterating her previous questions.

6 pm looms, and Oliva hasn't opened her previous message. Her stress intensifies once more as the clock ticks by. 9 pm arrives, and sleep eludes her; he *still* hasn't read her message. She tries ringing him, but there's no answer. Realizing she can't handle this alone, she calls Marcus.

Being the good friend he is, he swiftly arrives, realizing that it isn't the time for "I told you so." Tamara ushers him in and blurts out the whole story, a garbled mess of frantic anxiety. "He's married," Marcus asserts.

"What?! He's not! He told me he's divorced and looking to meet someone," Tamara vehemently defends him.

Marcus chuckles at her innocence, then shares a similar story of a friend of his. "Call him," he declares.

Tamara tries again, but still nothing. As midnight arrives, Marcus leaves, and Tamara clings to the hope that she has already fallen asleep, and that this is just a nightmare. She messages again, but more frantically: 'Hey, I'm begging you, for the sake of the moments we shared, could you please tell me what's wrong..." She then buries herself beneath the covers and falls into a disturbed sleep.

The next morning, she scrabbles around in the dark for her phone, and almost cries with relief to see a message from Oliva. But as she opens it, she realizes that something is wrong. The message reads, "Hey, I am so sorry for the late reply—I've been very busy. I think you're an amazing woman and believe you deserve the best, but I just don't think I'm right for you. Hope you find happiness because you truly deserve it. Take care, bye."

Each word strikes Tamara's chest like a dagger. *This has to be a dream…no, a nightmare.'* She dials him but like a sledgehammer, the noise hits her: she's been blocked.

She immediately calls Marcus, who comes straight round again, ever faithful. She stares at him, numb, refusing to accept this as her fate. *'The universe can't give you something so beautiful, then just take it back.'*

"I have to get him back," she declares.

"You need to move on," replies bluntly, giving her the bitter truth. "You've got lots going for you, a good career, films to make..."

"I want him *back!*" Tamara insists, refusing to accept rejection. *'This doesn't happen to me. It can't. I'll get him back. I know it.'*

Chapter 8: I Can't Breathe

In the silent depths of the night, Tamara finds herself caught in the throes of desperation. The painful days since the breakup have dragged by, her refusal to accept her fate hardening even as her resolve weakens. She blames herself; she must have gone wrong somewhere, said something wrong...

Clearly, she has become more attached to Oliva than she realized and now, the more she deepens her desperation to win him back, the more attached she becomes. She feels her self-esteem lessen with each passing moment; she is supposed to do the rejecting, not the other way round.

She turns to the digital oracle – Google – and types in the desperate plea, "How to get him back." Her world has crumbled around her, and she has abandoned her ongoing work. She hasn't spoken to anyone for days. In this abyss of despair, she still clings to the belief that a solution exists.

Google responds promptly, leading her into a labyrinth of articles, videos, and forums. From one result, a glimmer of hope appears: Psychic Zara. The text boasts of proven magical powers that can reunite lost lovers. Driven by a potent mix of desperation and hope, Tamara impulsively exchanges $500 for a virtual meeting with this stranger who claims mastery over the mystical forces of love.

As she anticipates the appointment, the weight of expectation hangs heavy. Rejection is not a language she has learned to speak, having resolved so strongly not to experience the 'Richard situation' again. No, she will find a way this time. She settles into the session, yearning for the magical revelation that will restore her lost love. Psychic Zara, however, begins with a few cryptic assurances about Tamara's great future. Disappointment creeps in; that's not why she's there.

After a few minutes, though, the psychic attempts to shift the focus. "To get him back, you must first understand your own strength," she utters, delving into a vague narrative of cosmic energies, soul connections, and personal power.

With every passing moment, Tamara's scepticism grows. The $500 becomes an afterthought as she grapples with the realization that the magic she sought might be nothing more than elusive promises wrapped in mystical mumbo-jumbo. The session concludes with a promise of future clarity, but instead it leaves her in a state of conflicted hope and lingering doubt.

As she exits Psychic Zara's virtual realm, disappointment weighs heavy on Tamara's shoulders. The anticipation that fueled her has transformed into a bitter acknowledgment – the magic she sought remains intangible, lost in a world of vague assurances. The journey to reclaim her love, it seems, is mired in uncertainty, and Tamara is left to navigate the shadows of disillusionment.

Undeterred by the disappointment, though, she dives deeper into the realm of mystical solutions. Night after night, she opens her wallet, exchanging dollars for glimpses into an elusive future where love is rekindled. The cycle repeats – another psychic, another session, another payment.

Each virtual visit paints a different picture, with cosmic brushstrokes weaving intricate tales of destiny, energies, and the ethereal connection between souls. Tamara, in her relentless pursuit, clings to the hope that the next one will hold the key, that the next reading will unravel the mystery of reclaiming what was lost.

But as the sessions accumulate, so does her disillusionment. Each payment becomes a painful reminder of her desperate quest for a solution, doubling the weight of her pain. All that is left behind is the dim realization that perhaps the answers she seeks lie not in the cosmic predictions of faceless strangers, but in the quiet resilience of her own spirit.

Faltering, she resolves to give one more a try—Psychic Tara. As she nervously awaits her appointment, the air in the room is thick with the weight of her expectations, a heavy cloak of hope that she clings to desperately. With a sense of trepidation, she settles into the session, yearning for the elusive revelation that promises to mend the fragments of her shattered love.

Psychic Tara, however, starts the encounter with advice about letting go, a narrative that doesn't align with Tamara's desperate quest for restoration. Disappointment creeps in immediately, casting shadows over the anticipation that had filled the room. This isn't what she came for – not some vague prophecy, but a roadmap back to the love she once had.

Yet, Psychic Tara, seemingly attuned to Tamara's unspoken needs, steers the conversation in a direction she didn't anticipate. "Why exactly do you want to get back a man who treated you with such disrespect?" The question hangs in the air for a few seconds, but it then hits Tamara like an unexpected gust of wind.

The response is a moment of truth, a revelation she's been avoiding even as it lingered beneath the surface. As the minutes tick by, each word from Psychic Tara delves deeper into Tamara's shadows, illuminating the painful truth she had concealed from herself. The session becomes a journey inward, a confrontation with the reality she's been reluctant to acknowledge.

"Why exactly do you want to get him back, Tamara?" Psychic Tara repeats, a gentle yet persistent guide through the labyrinth of Tamara's emotions.

"Because…" she starts, her voice barely a whisper as she grapples with the bitter truth that has been haunting her.

"Because what?"

"Because…" She hesitates, the words still caught in her throat, fighting an unwillingness to face the raw vulnerability within her.

"I can't handle rejection." The confession bursts forth, accompanied by a few tears that then allow the floodgates to open, pouring forth the flaws she's never dared to voice. In that moment, the room becomes a sacred space for the unraveling of her soul, laying bare the wounds she had long kept hidden from the world, and herself.

"This is what you need to work on," Psychic Tara concludes. "This is how you heal and grow."

Tamara feels an unsettling void, as if something vital has been sucked from her soul. The need for solitude becomes palpable, a necessity to reflect and grapple with the profound questions now echoing in her mind.

What is the origin of this fear of rejection that has taken residence within her? It's a puzzle she must solve, and she retreats into isolation, closing all her doors and blinds and methodically erasing her digital presence, starting with social media accounts. The room, once vibrant with life, morphs into a dim cocoon, shielding her from the outside world. Answers are what she seeks.

In the blurred continuum of days and nights, she succumbs to the weightiness within her. Time becomes an inconsequential notion, and the world outside fades into a distant, muted echo. Amidst the solitude, Tamara embarks on a quest for answers. Each question she poses to herself brings her a step closer to unraveling the mystery shrouded in her heart.

Her room, now a sanctuary for self-discovery, harbors relics of her past – family photos, cherished stories, and mementos scattered across the place. As she delves into the troves of memories, each item becomes a gateway to revelations. The echo of laughter in some photos, the narratives interwoven with joy and sorrow – it becomes a mirror that simply reflects the complexities of her soul.

The process is emotional, a cathartic excavation of buried emotions. She grapples with the shadows that have shaped her, seeking solace in the understanding of her own vulnerabilities. The cocoon of isolation becomes one of introspection, and in the dusk of her room, she is not just seeking answers; she is forging a path toward self-acceptance and healing.

Chapter 9: Not So Fast

Alone in her bedroom, Tamara crumbles onto the plush bed. The air thickens as she gasps for breath, and the muffled sobs escape her and pierce the silence, each one a poignant note of mourning and shattered dreams.

Determined to sever the emotional ties that bind her, she reaches for her phone, her fingers moving with purpose. With each deliberate swipe, she deletes all traces of Oliva – every tender text message, every shared moment, every picture. This digital catharsis serves as a deliberate, symbolic gesture to reclaim control over her broken heart. With each deletion, she gathers up a piece, with each passing moment she glues herself back together.

As the night descends, casting long shadows across the room, she finds herself locked in a restless struggle for sleep, tossing and turning on the battleground of her bed. The soft glow of the moonlight filtering through the curtains paints a scene of turmoil.

Moving from one side to the other, she exchanges pillows in a futile search for comfort. But frustration, her close companion, accompanies her and urges her to sit up and confront the lingering echoes of the past. With a determined sigh, she opens her phone once more, a beacon of connection to the memories she longs to erase.

In a moment of vulnerability, she finds herself beginning the painstaking task of recovering all deleted text messages and photos of Oliva from her phone's digital abyss. Each recovered memory is a double-edged sword, invoking both pain and longing. She opens a link from his past messages, clicks, and a haunting melody begins to play – a song that once carried shared laughter and stolen glances.

Initially, she listens to it cheerfully, lost in the bittersweet nostalgia. The room resonates with the echoes of a love now lost. But then, an abrupt realization causes her to abruptly bring it to a halt. With resolve anew, she presses onward, resuming her purging mission.

Deleting all these messages and photos over again delivers a therapeutic ritual, a second digital exorcism to expel the remnants of a love now turned bitter. With relentless determination, she goes one step further, emptying digital recycling bins and completely wiping away any last trace of him, putting an end to pull of weakness.

That book, too, and its promises of manifesting a "dream man" must go. She tosses it into the fire and watches the metaphor for recovery take hold, licking its way around the words and cleansing her soul. Then, she removes the dating app from her phone, it, too, having acted as a silent accomplice to her heartache. *No reminders, no triggers.'*

She turns out the light and slips under the covers, her room now cloaked in darkness. The ensuing night is a tempest of emotions, but as the darkness deepens, so does her resolve. There, in the quiet solitude of her room, she takes a deliberate breath, finding solace in the realization that, despite the pain, she possesses the strength to move forward.

As sleep claims her and wraps her in a cocoon of temporary peace, the promise of a new dawn whispers in the shadows. It assures her that the echoes of this past chapter will fade and be replaced by the unwritten pages of a future untethered by the weight of lost love.

Chapter 10: Your Name Again?

inally free from the shackles she placed upon herself, Tamara embraces her true self once again. She lets go of the fleeting fantasy of staying sexy and slim and finds contentment in the simplicity of her routine – work, life, and her favorite foods. Weight loss is no longer a pressing concern; she's happy just the way she is. The prospect of finding love, or even something more casual, becomes less of an emphasis - a delightful miracle if it comes along, but not an issue if it doesn't.

But in the midst of this delightfully mundane normalcy, an unexpected interruption arrives. She receives an email notification – someone has messaged her on the app. She opens the email and lingers on it for a while before shrugging casually, heading to her phone settings, and turning off the notification button. *'Lesson learned, no more interruptions, no more surprises.'*

The weeks roll by, but while Tamara has grown stronger in routine, there is a tinge of boredom to her existence that causes her to revisit that small seed of lingering curiosity. She navigates to her app store and downloads the dating app once again. *Just a peek – just to see…* 'To her surprise, several messages await her, all from the same persistent soul. He has been busy, sending out weekly communications in the hope of a response. A mischievous glint sparkles in Tamara's eyes. *'Alright then, let's play games,'* she thinks to herself with a sly grin.

Copying the messages, she tosses them into the realm of artificial intelligence, instructing it to craft a response. A few seconds later, she sends the AI-generated reply back to the persistent sender. She couldn't care less. She retires for the night, leaving the ball firmly in his court.

The next morning, she wakes up to a message – if you can call a novella a message. She rolls her eyes. *'Seriously, does he expect me to read one of these every day?'* She scans the message and notes the first line – a seemingly innocent request for her to share more about herself. *'Alright then, see how you handle this!'* She pulls out the big guns straight away and sends him her CV bio, a written testament to her achievements. *'Choke on this.'*

Several weeks fly by, but this new Romeo persists. Like clockwork, he sends a message every day, each one continuing for several paragraphs Tamara, however, remains unimpressed. These marathon monologues only serve as a reminder of her past, especially the eerily familiar 'good morning' lines that trigger memories of Oliva's similar routine.

Ever the sceptic, she starts to wonder if there is a secret guidebook for persistent suitors, one that this guy is following to the letter. One message a day, regardless of her response – it's a pattern that both annoys and intrigues her. *'What's the catch?'*

Unable to contain her curiosity, she spills the beans to Marcus, her trusted confidant in matters of the heart.

As she shows him the messages, Marcus is visibly taken aback. "Good Lord, is he writing a novel or confessing his sins?" he exclaims, bursting into laughter.

"It's insane, right?" she responds, equally amused and perplexed.

"But then again, he is investing real quality time here," Marcus then observes, conceding a hint of respect for the substance of the communication.

"And?" Tamara queries, sensing there's more to his deduction.

"You only invest time in something or someone you care about," he adds.

"Get to the point," Tamara urges.

"He likes you."

"Stop it," Tamara scoffs, attempting to brush off the notion.

"No, really. Despite the odd method, this guy seems genuine. He's investing time to get to know you."

Tamara crosses her arms defensively. "Not interested," she asserts.

"Why not give him a shot? Go on one date with him," Marcus suggests, grinning mischievously.

Tamara chuckles in amusement. "You're enjoying this way too much."

"Just think about it," he adds. "Who knows, he might surprise you."

She doesn't have long to wait for the opportunity. Only a few days later, the man, clearly emboldened by her replies, requests a date. Tamara toils over Marcus's words, but eventually agrees. She doesn't expect much, but supposes that if nothing else, she can cash in on a decent meal.

On the day of the much-anticipated dinner, Tamara steps into the restaurant embodying a sense of casual authenticity. Her choice of attire mirrors her genuine self, without the embellishments of makeup or the formality of an evening gown. She is relaxed, unbothered. *This isn't a display, nor is it a performance.'* Instead, she decides to present herself in her most unfiltered form.

As she scans the bustling restaurant for her date, a flicker of doubt flits across her mind. Will he match the expectations she unknowingly crafted in her imagination? She has deliberately avoided becoming desperate, attending with an open heart not to seek perfection, but connection.

Standing by the entrance, a Caucasian man catches her eye. He is tall, unassumingly average in appearance, with a confident demeanor that speaks of self-assurance. He seems to exude an understated charm, a quality that Tamara begins to appreciate as she observes him from a distance. It's not an immediate attraction; rather, a slow recognition of the authenticity in his presence.

Jeremy stands tall - not quite Oliva's height - but with a stature that holds a commanding presence. His broad chest creates a comforting embrace, wide enough to cocoon Tamara in a sense of security. His unmasked features, visibly genuine and bold, reveal a man comfortable in his own skin. But most striking is his charming smile, accompanied by an intriguing quality that unfolds with each observation, though it is too early for Tamara to see it yet. When he smiles, authenticity radiates through his eyes, leaving an indelible impression of sincerity and warmth. She catches his gaze and waves him over, sure of herself and comfortable in her own skin.

"What was your name again?" she asks as he arrives. He is clearly a bit taken aback but responds with a smile and shrugs it off. "Jeremy. Lovely to meet you, Tamara." Then, he walks around the table and pulls her chair back for her, waiting for her to sit before taking his own. As they settle into the surroundings, Tamara finds time to appreciate the chivalrous gesture, the kind act sending a ripple through her thoughts. Jeremy may not look like a model, but he certainly exudes enough confidence and charm to be attractive.

Nevertheless, she remains vigilant, reminding herself of past experiences and the knowledge that the depths of a man's heart can be elusive, holding mysteries beyond perception.

The ambiance of the restaurant envelops them as the evening unfolds, the clinking of glasses and the gentle hum of conversations creating a backdrop for their shared experience. In no time, the wine arrives, followed by a delightful array of dishes, concluding with a small, sweet dessert. Throughout the culinary journey, their conversation flows seamlessly. To an onlooker, the dialog may have appeared business-like, as Tamara passionately shares her love for film, and Jeremy sits quietly, listening attentively.

The night air is cool as they step out of the restaurant, their breath visible in the crisp air. Jeremy walks her to her car, the dim glow of the streetlights casting a soft aura around them. Despite the evening's events, she dismisses him with a quick nod - no hug, no lingering moments. As she starts her car and drives away, the engine's hum is drowned out by the swirl of thoughts in her mind.

The familiar streetlights flicker overhead, casting intermittent shadows on the road. Tamara can't help but replay some of their conversations in her head. She smirks as she recalls Jeremy's attempt at humor and the way he confidently navigated through their dinner chat. A smile creeps across her face, but just as quickly as it appears, she shakes it off.

"Never again," she mutters to herself, trying to quell the rising warmth in her chest. She navigates through the quiet streets, the occasional passing car leaving streaks of light in her rear-view mirror.

She glances at her phone, tempted to send a message to Marcus. *'Should I tell him it wasn't a disaster?'* she wonders, then shakes her head. The idea of dissecting every detail with him feels too revealing.

As the city lights twinkle in the distance, she takes a deep breath. The evening wasn't what she had expected. Jeremy, with his unconventional approach to messaging and genuine interest, had managed to surprise her. Despite her attempts to dismiss the date as just another experiment, a small part of her acknowledges that there might be more to explore.

The remainder of the car ride home is accompanied by a mix of thoughts, a cacophony of emotions. At one point, she catches herself chuckling at something Jeremy said, a genuine and unguarded laugh that escapes her lips. She clutches the steering wheel, realizing that maybe, just maybe, this unexpected rendezvous could hold the promise of a new chapter—one she hadn't anticipated.

Parking in her driveway, she turns off the engine, the quiet hum of the car replaced by the stillness of the night. She sits for a moment, staring at her house and contemplating the evening's events. With a sigh, she grabs her bag and steps out of the car, ready to face whatever twists and turns the new unpredictable journey might throw her way.

Chapter 11: 'The One'

The following day, as Tamara goes about her routine, she finds herself glancing at her phone more frequently than usual. The persistent messages from Jeremy no longer feel like a nuisance; instead, they have become a source of genuine anticipation. His words, once monotonous, now echo with a hint of familiarity that brings comfort.

As time ticks by, each passing minute contributes to a new tapestry, and the digital exchanges between Tamara and Jeremy seamlessly transition into the tangible richness of real-life connections. Jeremy surprises her by sharing a profound affection for the same quirky movies that have always held a special place in her heart.

Their conversations become a symphony of laughter, witty banter, and an unexpected connection that sparks something profound within her. As the layers unfold, it becomes apparent that they share more than just a love for peculiar films. Jeremy's character reveals a deep passion for his career, mirroring Tamara's own commitment and tenacity.

But this synergy extends beyond professional pursuits to shared laughter—a mutual exchange where Jeremy finds himself caught in the charm of Tamara's jokes, reciprocated by her own laughter echoing through the air in response to his wit. It's as if Tamara has discovered her own latent talent for comedy, brought to light by this effortless that they share.

Tamara realizes that her connection with Jeremy goes beyond just looks or interests. To her, he's not just a person; he's like a kindred spirit, a soul that resonates with hers. This feeling brings her a deep sense of satisfaction, making their connection even more special and fulfilling.

One day, as the sun sets in hues of warm oranges and pinks, she finds herself in a cozy coffee shop with Jeremy. The air is filled with the comforting aroma of freshly brewed coffee, and as they talk, she understands that she has discovered his realness—a quality she cherishes. He doesn't sugar-coat his experiences or pretend to be someone he's not. His authenticity resonates with her, creating a bond that feels refreshingly genuine. Having experienced the opposite, she not only finds herself able to spot these qualities, but to appreciate them as well.

As their connection deepens, she reflects on her past involvement with Oliva. Perhaps what she had perceived as a profound connection was, in reality, nothing more than a fleeting infatuation driven by appearances. The contrast with Jeremy's genuine efforts to understand and connect with her becomes more apparent, serving as an important reminder of the importance of substance over superficial allure.

Jeremy's authenticity shines through as much in what he says as in what he does. He not only listens to Tamara but truly hears her, attuning himself to the nuances of her heartbeat. This is evident in the little things, such as willingly watching her favorite movie, delving into the books she holds dear, and choosing her cherished places as locations for outings. It's a stark contrast to the superficial connection she now realizes that she had with Oliva.

Jeremy's other qualities emerge bit by bit. He's not just a lawyer; he's a handyman around her house, a willing helper with her shopping, a companion to her needs. Gradually, his deeds are proudly displayed like badges of honour around Tamara's home. His proficiency in these day-to-day tasks not only adds practical value but also reveals his thoughtful side even further as he solidifies his place in their lives through his benevolent actions.

Their connection deepens, and Tamara finds solace in the stability he brings to her life. He embraces her true self with open arms, appreciating the genuine laughter that fills their shared moments. She forgets the shallow dream of staying sexy and slim for a tall, handsome model of a man; the real goal is an authentic connection that transcends societal expectations and celebrates the shared joy of being unapologetically themselves.

One evening, after a delicious dinner of roast pork, Tamara senses that the atmosphere is tense and charged with anticipation. She is caught off guard and slightly uneasy for the first time in a long time. A moment hangs in the air as Jeremy takes a deep breath, but then he stands and kneels before her, excitement gleaming in his eyes.

With a sparkling diamond ring between his fingers, he declares, "Marry me." Tamara's heart races, and she feels the joy bubbling up inside her. Tears cascade down her cheeks and she smiles and leans forward. "Jeremy, this is a wonderful gesture. Thank you." She hesitates before continuing, but then adds, "But I don't want to rush. I love being with you, but it's too soon. I hope you understand."

Despite sensing that he might be "The One," she has learned from her past experiences. Her encounter with Oliva has taught her not to rush and avoid hasty conclusions. She now knows that truly understanding a person takes time, and she is in no hurry. If it takes a lifetime to unravel the intricacies of Jeremy or anyone else, she is willing to invest that time.

Jeremy smiles, appreciating the honesty. Her sentiments are clear, and he, too, is willing to wait for as long as she needs, understanding the value of patience in building a lasting connection. As they embrace, the tension in the room transforms into a different kind of anticipation, one that speaks of a journey to be taken, an understanding to be deepened, and a connection to be nurtured over time.

In that moment, Tamara realizes that sometimes, love doesn't come in a neat, predictable package. It arrives in quirky messages, shared laughter, and genuine conversations. Her past, once so damaging to her, is replaced by the unwritten pages of a future bursting with love, laughter, and the promise of a connection that is truly as real as it gets.

Her journey with Jeremy is a deliberate exploration, a patient unfolding of shared experiences. They can both take the time to allow their connection to grow organically, nurturing it with the care and consideration that true connections deserve. Together, they have found a sense of peace and wisdom, and Tamara revels in knowing that the depth of a connection is best discovered over time. After all, why rush? True love is a journey, not a destination.